RORY
and his
Great Idea

Author: Andrew Wolffe   Illustrator: Tom Cole

Text and illustrations copyright©, Keppel Publishing, 2003.
The Rory Stories is a Registered Trademark of Keppel Publishing.
This edition published 2003.
ISBN: 0 9534949 5 0

A CIP catalogue record for this book is available from the British Library.

Printed in Singapore

Keppel Publishing Ltd.
The Grey House, Kenbridge Road,
New Galloway, DG7 3RP, Scotland.

It was another lovely day in Sandy Bay. All summer long there hadn't been a cloud in the blue sky and the temperature had soared. Rory and Scruff McDuff were sitting on a sand dune enjoying a picnic.

Soon they had eaten all the tasty sandwiches that Rory's Mum had made for them and finished a very large portion of delicious strawberries. Rory had drunk the last of his juice and not a drop of water was left in Scruff McDuff's bowl. But they were both still thirsty and feeling hot.

Suddenly a friendly voice rang out across the sand.

"Ahoy there, Rory lad, spotted anything unusual out at sea?" Rory and Scruff McDuff turned round to see their friend, Captain Campbell, striding towards them.

"There have been reports of something strange drifting towards Sandy Bay," the Captain continued as he lifted his telescope to his eyes and started to scan the horizon.

"We haven't seen anything yet, Captain Campbell, but now that we know we'll be on the look out," Rory promised.

"You do that lads and let me know as soon as you see anything unusual," he said with a smile. "Best thing in weather like this is a visit to the Pelican Café," Captain Campbell advised as he tucked his telescope under his arm and continued on his way along the shore.

"Why didn't we think of that?" Rory asked Scruff McDuff, as he dug into his pocket. "I forgot Mum gave me some money for ice cream cones. Let's pack up quickly. We can hide our picnic basket and come back for it later."

ortunately they didn't have far to walk in the heat. The Pelican Café stands at the top of the path from the beach. As they drew nearer they were delighted to see that there wasn't the usual long queue of people standing outside.

"I want lots of raspberry sauce on my ice cream," Rory said, smiling at the thought of his treat.

"Do you want chocolate sauce as usual Scruff McDuff?" Rory's little friend wagged his tail and licked his lips in response.

But when they walked inside the Café and reached the counter, instead of refreshing ice cream cones there was an unpleasant surprise waiting for Rory and Scruff McDuff.

"Sorry my friends," Mr Toni, the Café's owner, said sadly. "No ice cream today."

"No ice cream!" Rory gasped in disbelief, as Scruff McDuff's tail dropped to the floor in disappointment at the terrible news. "But Mr Toni, the Pelican Café always has ice cream."

"I know, it's the first time it's ever happened," Mr Toni said, mopping his brow. "My freezer and ice machine have been working so hard in the hot weather that they have broken down. To make matters worse, my cold drinks are getting warmer by the minute."

"I wish we could do something to help Mr Toni but it's too hot to think," Rory said to Scruff McDuff as they slowly made their way back to the beach.

Just then, a pair of puffins flew past.
"How do you manage to keep cool when it's so hot?" Rory called up to them.

"We take to the air and free-wheel in the sea breeze, like this...

...and this...

...and sometimes, we even do this - WHEE!" replied one of the puffins as he did a perfect loop the loop.

Rory was still deep in thought wondering what they could do to help Mr Toni, when he suddenly noticed what looked like a large white rock glistening out in the bay.

"What do you think that is, Scruff McDuff?"
Rory asked, dazzled by its brightness. "I think
we'd better go and find Captain Campbell."

"It's an iceberg, Rory, a great big iceberg," Captain Campbell replied as he stood on top of a rock, inspecting the enormous block of ice through his telescope. "I never thought I would see one in these parts. Last time one crossed my bow was in the frozen northern seas. It was so cold, I had icicles hanging from my beard."

The iceberg was so white, it almost hurt Rory's eyes to stare at it. "A huge lump of ice like that must be very cold," he said aloud. Then a really great idea popped into Rory's head.

"Captain Campbell," he said excitedly. "Why don't we sail out to the iceberg and bring back some of it for Mr Toni?"

Luckily Captain Campbell, who was also very fond of ice cream, thought it was a terrific suggestion. Together Rory, Scruff McDuff and the Captain quickly made their way to Sandy Bay harbour to fill Captain Campbell's boat with as many empty buckets as they could find.

The iceberg seemed even bigger once the boat sailed alongside. Rory and Captain Campbell worked hard for a long time, chipping away blocks of ice for the Pelican Café. Scruff McDuff, meanwhile, took the chance to cool down by licking the iceberg every so often with very noisy slurps!

"That's enough frozen cargo for this trip," declared Captain Campbell when all the buckets were full. "We can always come back for more."

When Rory and Scruff McDuff returned to the Pelican Café with all the buckets of ice, they were given a heroes' welcome.

"Cold drinks on the house and ice cream cones as soon as they're ready," announced a delighted Mr Toni. "Three cheers for Rory and Scruff McDuff!"